WONDERFUL YOU

Library of Congress Cataloging-in-Publication Data

Burstein, John.
       The spirit / by Slim Goodbody ; illustrated by Terry Boles.
            p.   cm. — (Wonderful you)
       Summary: Explores the concept of the human spirit.
       ISBN 1-57749-016-9
       1. Spirit. 2. Mind and body. [1. Spirit. 2. Mind and body.] I. Boles, Terry, ill. II. Title.
III. Series: Wonderful you (Minneapolis, Minn.)
      BD421.B87   1996
      128'.1—dc20   96-8285
                                                    CIP
                                                    AC

Cover design by Barry Littmann.

First Printing: September 1996
Printed in the United States of America

00 99 98 97 96   7 6 5 4 3 2 1

Published by Fairview Press, 2450 Riverside Avenue South, Minneapolis, MN 55454.

For a current catalog of Fairview Press titles, please call this Toll-Free number: 1-800-544-8207

Publisher's Note: Fairview Press publishes books and other materials related to the subjects of family and social issues. Its publications, including *The Spirit,* do not necessarily reflect the philosophy of Fairview Hospital and Healthcare Services or their treatment programs.

The paper used in this publication meets the minimum requirements of American National Standard for Information Sciences—Permanence of Paper for Printed Library Materials, ANSI Z329.48-1984.

THE SPIRIT

Slim Goodbody

illustrated by Terry Boles

Fairview Press
Minneapolis

You have a body,
You have a mind,
And one other part
A bit harder to find.

An invisible force,
Not meant for seeing,
That lies deep within
At the core of your being.

But if you listen closely,
Sometimes you can hear it.
A small loving voice
Inside you—your spirit.

It's a spirit of love,
Of joy and of giving,
A spirit revealing
The lessons for living.

As you grow older,
This spirit inside you
Will lovingly help you,
Teach you and guide you.

For some people, spirit is a small inner voice. For others, it's a special feeling. Your spirit helps make you the person you are and helps you become the wise and caring person you want to be.

Sometimes you *feel* your spirit when—
You see something so beautiful that it makes you feel wonderfully special inside—happy and sad at the same time, and really glad to be alive.

Sometimes you *hear* your spirit when—
You ask for help in making a decision and the right answer seems to "come to you."

Think About

👁 Have you ever felt or heard your own spirit? How did it make you feel?

Where inside
Does spirit reside?

It's everywhere and every place,
Behind the smile on your face,
In your fingers, in your hair,
Spirit's flowing everywhere.
In your blood and your heart,
Your spirit's part of every part.

Your spirit is different from your body and mind, but it's not separate from them. You can think of spirit as an energy force that flows within. It's something like a wave in the sea. The wave isn't separate from the water—it simply gives motion to the ocean.

There are different ways to get in touch with your spirit. Here's one you can try:

In a quiet place,
Sit or lie in a comfortable way.
Close your eyes,
Let your body relax,
And then stay very still.
Breathe in and out easily,
Quiet your thoughts,
Get very, very peaceful,
And listen to what your spirit says.

Think About

👀 Even though your spirit flows everywhere inside you, many people feel it very strongly in their heart. Why do you think that is?

You can't see the air,
But it's there.
The spirit in you
Is invisible, too.

The English word *spirit* comes from a Latin word *spiritus,* which means *breath.* In Greek the word for spirit is *pneuma,* and in Hebrew it's *rauch.* Both these words also mean breath or wind. That's because spirit and breath have two very important things in common—they are both invisible and necessary for life.

Think About

⌾ Another word for breathing is "reSPIRation." What word can you almost see? Why do you think it's there?

9

To life,
Your spirit gives birth,
Like the warmth of the sun
Brings life to the earth.

Your spirit is a life-giving force flowing through each and every part of your being. You can compare it to the electricity that makes a light bulb shine. Without power, there's darkness. But when the current is flowing, the light is glowing.

Think About

☙ When people die, it's as if their "light" goes out. Their bodies don't disappear—they're still there. But something is definitely missing. What do you think it is?

☙ Suppose a person has lost a leg or is blind. Would his or her spirit be decreased (lessened)? Does spirit depend upon the body for its strength, or does the body depend on the spirit?

11

Life-giving spirit,
Shining inside,
An inner teacher,
A loving guide.

If you listen and pay attention, your spirit will teach how to be the best person you can be—by being true to yourself. Being true to yourself means doing the things you know are right.

Think About

👀 People say that when you're true to yourself, you grow strong in your spirit and your spirit grows strong in you. What do you think that means?

The most important thing, by far,
Is not what you have,
But who you are.
Not what you look like,
Not what you wear.
But are you loving?
Do you care?

Your spirit helps you decide which values are truly valuable and which are not. Values are what you believe in, deep down inside. What you believe in causes you to make decisions about what to do and how to act. Each day you can do things that are helpful or harmful, positive or negative. It all depends upon what you value the most.

Think About

👀 Some of the values your spirit may encourage are caring, sharing, loving-kindness, being fair and honest, keeping promises, and telling the truth. Why do you think these values are important?

Your spirit sings a sad, sad song
When you do things you know are wrong.
It sings with joy and great delight
When you do things you know are right.

Doing what's right isn't always easy, but it's always important. If you do something that's wrong, especially when you know better, you'll feel bad inside. That's one of the ways your spirit guides you. And if you're truly sorry, and ask for guidance, your spirit will help you figure out what to do to make things better. Remember, your spirit always loves you, but it may not like some of the things that you do.

Think About

◬ What are some of the things your spirit tells you not to do? Why?

17

To grow in understanding,
Keep an open mind.
Be curious and question,
Seek, and you will find.

The whole world is a teacher
For people who are wise,
Who know to see things with their heart
And not just with their eyes.

You can learn something from just about everyone and everything. A dog can teach you about loyalty, and a tree can teach you about standing strong. Flowers reveal how nature moves in cycles, from birth to death to new birth. A stream of water proves that being soft will wear down and smooth even the roughest stones.

Think About

👀 Were you ever surprised to learn a lesson when you least expected it? What was the lesson? What taught it to you?

The Spirit Says

Nobody's perfect.
Everyone makes
All kinds of different
And silly mistakes.

Each time you make one,
Your major concern
Should be the lesson
You're able to learn.

You don't need to be perfect. You're wonderful
just the way you are. If you fail, don't give up.
Start in again tomorrow. Failure is when you stop trying.

Think About

👀 You can sometimes mistake your idea of what
is right, for what is right. Have you ever insisted
you were correct and then later on realized that
maybe you weren't? How did you feel?

The Spirit Says

Be grateful for all
Of life's gifts,
Sunlight and rainbows,
And giant snowdrifts.

Cool streams for swimming,
Mountains to climb,
Breezes that blow
In the warm summertime.

Your spirit wants you to take time to appreciate all the wonderful things you've been given—your family, your friends, and the beautiful world you live in.

Think About

☙ What are some of the things, and who are some of the people, that you're most grateful for?

The Spirit Says

A little help, a little love,
Even small amounts,
Add up to make a better world,
'Cause every kindness counts.

When somebody does something good,
We are all affected.
'Cause every single one of us
In some way is connected.

Every time you do something nice or helpful, every time you do a good deed, every time you listen to and follow your spirit's prompting, you're making the world a little better place to live in. Every single action counts, even small ones.

Think About

👁 When you do something positive, like acting with kindness, you are setting an example for others. Then, if they do something kind, it sets an example for still more people. What would the world be like if everybody treated everybody else with loving-kindness?

The Spirit Says

There's a lesson for living,
Golden and true—
Treat others the way
You want them to treat you.

This is a lesson that's been taught and practiced for thousands and thousands of years. If you follow this teaching, it's one of the surest ways to know if you are acting in harmony with your spirit.

Think About

๑๑ Why do you think this is called the "Golden Rule"? How would the world be different if everyone practiced it?

The Spirit Says

One of the greatest
Secrets of living
Is the joy you receive
At the moment of giving.

When you give something to another with love in your heart, a funny thing happens. You get back something even more precious—a terrific feeling. It's almost as if the universe is sending you a thank-you note and a big warm hug.

Think About

👀 Giving doesn't always involve buying a present. You can give a hug, a kiss, a smile, or a kind word. There's an expression that says, "The best things in life are free." What do you think that means?

The Spirit Says

You do something wonderful
No one else can do—
That's to be the one and only
Very special you.

It's very, very important to your spirit that you remember to appreciate yourself. You are amazing—a unique and wondrous miracle of life. You're made up of the same materials that make up the stars!

Think About

👁 What does it mean to say that people are like snowflakes? What do all people have in common? What's different about us?

Cultivate your spirit
Like a garden, give it care.
Tend it with a welcome heart,
Nourish it with prayer.
Sow the seeds of kindness,
And be sure that you include
The bright sunshine of honesty,
Love and gratitude.

30

Nurture and nourish your spirit as it nurtures and nourishes you. That's the way to make your inner garden into a paradise. And remember, you can't force a flower to bloom. It blossoms when it's ready, in its own sweet time. Everything has its season. The universe, and all things within it, unfolds naturally.

Think About

👁 What are some of the things you do every day to help make your inner garden more and more beautiful?

Other children's books from Fairview Press

Alligator in the Basement, by Bob Keeshan, TV's Captain Kangaroo
illustrated by Kyle Corkum

Box-Head Boy, by Christine M. Winn with David Walsh, Ph.D.
illustrated by Christine M. Winn

Clover's Secret, by Christine M. Winn with David Walsh, Ph.D.
illustrated by Christine M. Winn

Hurry, Murray, Hurry!, by Bob Keeshan, TV's Captain Kangaroo
illustrated by Chad Peterson

Monster Boy, by Christine M. Winn with David Walsh, Ph.D.
illustrated by Christine M. Winn

My Dad Has HIV, by Earl Alexander, Sheila Rudin, Pam Sejkora
illustrated by Ronnie Walter Shipman

"Wonderful You" Series, by Slim Goodbody
illustrated by Terry Boles
The Body
The Mind
The Spirit